Boris Godunov: A Drama in Verse

Aleksandr Pushkin

Translated by Alfred Hayes

Esprios.com

BORIS GODUNOV

A Drama in Verse

By ALEXANDER PUSHKIN

Rendered into English verse by Alfred Hayes

DRAMATIS PERSONAE*

BORIS GODUNOV, afterwards Tsar.

PRINCE SHUISKY, Russian noble.

PRINCE VOROTINSKY, Russian noble.

SHCHELKALOV, Russian Minister of State.

FATHER PIMEN, an old monk and chronicler.

GREGORY OTREPIEV, a young monk, afterwards the Pretender

to the throne of Russia.

THE PATRIARCH, Abbot of the Chudov Monastery.

MISSAIL, wandering friar.

VARLAAM, wandering friar.

ATHANASIUS MIKAILOVICH PUSHKIN, friend of Prince Shuisky.

FEODOR, young son of Boris Godunov.

SEMYON NIKITICH GODUNOV, secret agent of Boris Godunov.

GABRIEL PUSHKIN, nephew of A. M. Pushkin.

PRINCE KURBSKY, disgraced Russian noble.

KHRUSHCHOV, disgraced Russian noble.

KARELA, a Cossack.

PRINCE VISHNEVETSKY.

MNISHEK, Governor of Sambor.

BASMANOV, a Russian officer.

MARZHERET, officer of the Pretender.

ROZEN, officer of the Pretender.

DIMITRY, the Pretender, formerly Gregory Otrepiev.

MOSALSKY, a Boyar.

KSENIA, daughter of Boris Godunov.

NURSE of Ksenia.

MARINA, daughter of Mnishek.

ROUZYA, tire-woman of Ksenia.

HOSTESS of tavern.

Boyars, The People, Inspectors, Officers, Attendants, Guests, a Boy in attendance on Prince Shuisky, a Catholic Priest, a Polish Noble, a Poet, an Idiot, a Beggar, Gentlemen, Peasants, Guards, Russian, Polish, and German Soldiers, a Russian Prisoner of War, Boys, an old Woman, Ladies, Serving-women.

*The list of Dramatis Personae which does not appear in the original has been added for the convenience of the reader—A. H.

Boris Godunov: A Drama in Verse

PALACE OF THE KREMLIN

(FEBRUARY 20th, A.D. 1598)

PRINCE SHUISKY and VOROTINSKY

VOROTINSKY. To keep the city's peace, that is the task Entrusted to us twain, but you forsooth Have little need to watch; Moscow is empty; The people to the Monastery have flocked After the patriarch. What thinkest thou? How will this trouble end?

SHUISKY. How will it end? That is not hard to tell. A little more The multitude will groan and wail, Boris Pucker awhile his forehead, like a toper Eyeing a glass of wine, and in the end Will humbly of his graciousness consent To take the crown; and then—and then will rule us Just as before.

VOROTINSKY. A month has flown already Since, cloistered with his sister, he forsook The world's affairs. None hitherto hath shaken His purpose, not the patriarch, not the boyars His counselors; their tears, their prayers he heeds not; Deaf is he to the wail of Moscow, deaf To the Great Council's voice; vainly they urged The sorrowful nun-queen to consecrate Boris to sovereignty; firm was his sister, Inexorable as he; methinks Boris Inspired her with this spirit. What if our ruler Be sick in very deed of cares of state And hath no strength to mount the throne? What Say'st thou?

SHUISKY. I say that in that case the blood in vain Flowed of the young tsarevich, that Dimitry Might just as well be living.

VOROTINSKY. Fearful crime! Is it beyond all doubt Boris contrived The young boy's murder?

SHUISKY. Who besides? Who else Bribed Chepchugov in vain? Who sent in secret The brothers Bityagovsky with Kachalov? Myself was sent to Uglich, there to probe This matter on the spot; fresh traces there I found; the whole town bore witness to the crime; With one accord the burghers all affirmed it; And with a single word, when I returned, I could have proved the secret villain's guilt.

VOROTINSKY. Why didst thou then not crush him?

SHUISKY. At the time, I do confess, his unexpected calmness, His shamelessness, dismayed me. Honestly He looked me in the eyes; he questioned me Closely, and I repeated to his face The foolish tale himself had whispered to me.

VOROTINSKY. An ugly business, prince.

SHUISKY. What could I do? Declare all to Feodor? But the tsar Saw all things with the eyes of Godunov, Heard all things with the ears of Godunov; Grant even that I might have fully proved it, Boris would have denied it there and then, And I should have been haled away to prison, And in good time—like mine own uncle—strangled Within the silence of some deaf-walled dungeon. I boast not when I say that, given occasion, No penalty affrights me. I am no coward, But also am no fool, and do not choose Of my free will to walk into a halter.

VOROTINSKY. Monstrous misdeed! Listen; I warrant you Remorse already gnaws the murderer; Be sure the blood of that same innocent child Will hinder him from mounting to the throne.

SHUISKY. That will not baulk him; Boris is not so timid! What honour for ourselves, ay, for all Russia! A slave of yesterday, a Tartar, son By marriage of Maliuta, of a hangman, Himself in soul a hangman, he to wear The crown and robe of Monomakh! —

VOROTINSKY. You are right; He is of lowly birth; we twain can boast A nobler lineage.

SHUISKY. Indeed we may!

VOROTINSKY. Let us remember, Shuisky, Vorotinsky Are, let me say, born princes.

SHUISKY. Yea, born princes, And of the blood of Rurik.

VOROTINSKY. Listen, prince; Then we, 'twould seem, should have the right to mount Feodor's throne.

SHUISKY. Rather than Godunov.

VOROTINSKY. In very truth 'twould seem so.

SHUISKY. And what then? If still Boris pursue his crafty ways, Let us contrive by skilful means to rouse The people. Let them turn from Godunov; Princes they have in plenty of their own; Let them from out their number choose a tsar.

VOROTINSKY. Of us, Varyags in blood, there are full many, But 'tis no easy thing for us to vie With Godunov; the people are not wont To recognise in us an ancient branch Of their old warlike masters; long already Have we our appanages forfeited, Long served but as lieutenants of the tsars, And he hath known, by fear, and love, and glory, How to bewitch the people.

SHUISKY. (Looking through a window.) He has dared, That's all — while we — Enough of this. Thou seest Dispersedly the people are returning. We'll go forthwith and learn what is resolved.

THE RED SQUARE

THE PEOPLE

1ST PERSON. He is inexorable! He thrust from him Prelates, boyars, and Patriarch; in vain Prostrate they fall; the splendour of the throne Affrights him.

2ND PERSON. O, my God, who is to rule us? O, woe to us!

3RD PERSON. See! The Chief Minister Is coming out to tell us what the Council Has now resolved.

THE PEOPLE. Silence! Silence! He speaks, The Minister of State. Hush, hush! Give ear!

SHCHELKALOV. (From the Red Balcony.) The Council have resolved for the last time To put to proof the power of supplication Upon our ruler's mournful soul. At dawn, After a solemn service in the Kremlin, The blessed Patriarch will go, preceded By sacred banners, with the holy ikons Of Donsky and Vladimir; with him go The Council, courtiers, delegates, boyars, And all the orthodox folk of Moscow; all Will go to pray once more the queen to pity Fatherless Moscow, and to consecrate Boris unto the crown. Now to your homes Go ye in peace: pray; and to Heaven shall rise The heart's petition of the orthodox.

(The PEOPLE disperse.)

Boris Godunov: A Drama in Verse

THE VIRGIN'S FIELD

THE NEW NUNNERY. The People.

1ST PERSON. To plead with the tsaritsa in her cell Now are they gone. Thither have gone Boris, The Patriarch, and a host of boyars.

2ND PERSON. What news?

3RD PERSON. Still is he obdurate; yet there is hope.

PEASANT WOMAN. (With a child.) Drat you! Stop crying, or else the bogie-man Will carry you off. Drat you, drat you! Stop crying!

1ST PERSON. Can't we slip through behind the fence?

2ND PERSON. Impossible! No chance at all! Not only is the nunnery Crowded; the precincts too are crammed with people. Look what a sight! All Moscow has thronged here. See! Fences, roofs, and every single storey Of the Cathedral bell tower, the church-domes, The very crosses are studded thick with people.

1ST PERSON. A goodly sight indeed!

2ND PERSON. What is that noise?

3RD PERSON. Listen! What noise is that? —The people groaned; See there! They fall like waves, row upon row— Again—again— Now, brother, 'tis our turn; Be quick, down on your knees!

THE PEOPLE. (On their knees, groaning and wailing.) Have pity on us, Our father! O, rule over us! O, be Father to us, and tsar!

1ST PERSON. (Sotto voce.) Why are they wailing?

2ND PERSON. How can we know? The boyars know well enough. It's not our business.

PEASANT WOMAN. (With child.) Now, what's this? Just when It ought to cry, the child stops crying. I'll show you! Here comes the bogie-man! Cry, cry, you spoilt one! (Throws it on the ground; the child screams.) That's right, that's right!

1ST PERSON. As everyone is crying, We also, brother, will begin to cry.

2ND PERSON. Brother, I try my best, but can't.

1ST PERSON. Nor I. Have you not got an onion?

2ND PERSON. No; I'll wet My eyes with spittle. What's up there now?

1ST PERSON. Who knows What's going on?

THE PEOPLE. The crown for him! He is tsar! He has yielded! —Boris! —Our tsar! —Long live Boris!

Boris Godunov: A Drama in Verse

THE PALACE OF THE KREMLIN

BORIS, PATRIARCH, Boyars

BORIS. Thou, father Patriarch, all ye boyars! My soul lies bare before you; ye have seen With what humility and fear I took This mighty power upon me. Ah! How heavy My weight of obligation! I succeed The great Ivans; succeed the angel tsar! — O Righteous Father, King Of kings, look down From Heaven upon the tears of Thy true servants, And send on him whom Thou hast loved, whom Thou Exalted hast on earth so wondrously, Thy holy blessing. May I rule my people In glory, and like Thee be good and righteous! To you, boyars, I look for help. Serve me As ye served him, what time I shared your labours, Ere I was chosen by the people's will.

BOYARS. We will not from our plighted oath depart.

BORIS. Now let us go to kneel before the tombs Of Russia's great departed rulers. Then Bid summon all our people to a feast, All, from the noble to the poor blind beggar. To all free entrance, all most welcome guests.

(Exit, the Boyars following.)

PRINCE VOROTINSKY. (Stopping Shuisky.) You rightly guessed.

SHUISKY. Guessed what?

VOROTINSKY. Why, you remember— The other day, here on this very spot.

SHUISKY. No, I remember nothing.

VOROTINSKY. When the people Flocked to the Virgin's Field, thou said'st—

SHUISKY. 'Tis not The time for recollection. There are times When I should counsel you not to remember, But even to forget. And for the rest, I sought but by feigned calumny to prove thee, The truelier to discern thy secret thoughts. But see! The people hail the tsar—my absence May be remarked. I'll join them.

VOROTINSKY. Wily courtier!

Boris Godunov: A Drama in Verse

NIGHT

Cell in the Monastery of Chudov (A. D. 1603)

FATHER PIMEN, GREGORY (sleeping)

PIMEN (Writing in front of a sacred lamp.) One more, the final record, and my annals Are ended, and fulfilled the duty laid By God on me a sinner. Not in vain Hath God appointed me for many years A witness, teaching me the art of letters; A day will come when some laborious monk Will bring to light my zealous, nameless toil, Kindle, as I, his lamp, and from the parchment Shaking the dust of ages will transcribe My true narrations, that posterity The bygone fortunes of the orthodox Of their own land may learn, will mention make Of their great tsars, their labours, glory, goodness— And humbly for their sins, their evil deeds, Implore the Saviour's mercy. —In old age I live anew; the past unrolls before me. — Did it in years long vanished sweep along, Full of events, and troubled like the deep? Now it is hushed and tranquil. Few the faces Which memory hath saved for me, and few The words which have come down to me; — the rest Have perished, never to return. —But day Draws near, the lamp burns low, one record more, The last. (He writes.)

GREGORY. (Waking.) Ever the selfsame dream! Is 't possible? For the third time! Accursed dream! And ever Before the lamp sits the old man and writes— And not all night, 'twould seem, from drowsiness, Hath closed his eyes. I love the peaceful sight, When, with his soul deep in the past immersed, He keeps his chronicle. Oft have I longed To guess what 'tis he writes of. Is 't perchance The dark dominion of the Tartars? Is it Ivan's grim punishments, the stormy Council of Novgorod? Is it about the glory Of our dear fatherland? —I ask in vain! Not on his lofty brow, nor in his looks May one peruse his secret thoughts; always The same aspect; lowly at once, and lofty— Like some state Minister grown grey in office, Calmly alike he contemplates the just And guilty, with indifference he hears Evil and good, and knows not wrath nor pity.

PIMEN. Wakest thou, brother?

GREGORY. Honoured father, give me Thy blessing.

PIMEN. May God bless thee on this day, Tomorrow, and for ever.

GREGORY. All night long Thou hast been writing and abstained from sleep, While demon visions have disturbed my peace, The fiend molested me. I dreamed I scaled By winding stairs a turret, from whose height Moscow appeared an anthill, where the people Seethed in the squares below and pointed at me With laughter. Shame and terror came upon me— And falling headlong, I awoke. Three times I dreamed the selfsame dream. Is it not strange?

PIMEN. 'Tis the young blood at play; humble thyself By prayer and fasting, and thy slumber's visions Will all be filled with lightness. Hitherto If I, unwillingly by drowsiness Weakened, make not at night long orisons, My old-man's sleep is neither calm nor sinless; Now riotous feasts appear, now camps of war, Scuffles of battle, fatuous diversions Of youthful years.

GREGORY. How joyfully didst thou Live out thy youth! The fortress of Kazan Thou fought'st beneath, with Shuisky didst repulse The army of Litva. Thou hast seen the court, And splendour of Ivan. Ah! Happy thou! Whilst I, from boyhood up, a wretched monk, Wander from cell to cell! Why unto me Was it not given to play the game of war, To revel at the table of a tsar? Then, like to thee, would I in my old age Have gladly from the noisy world withdrawn, To vow myself a dedicated monk, And in the quiet cloister end my days.

PIMEN. Complain not, brother, that the sinful world Thou early didst forsake, that few temptations The All-Highest sent to thee. Believe my words; The glory of the world, its luxury, Woman's seductive love, seen from afar, Enslave our souls. Long have I lived, have taken Delight in many things, but never knew True bliss until that season when the Lord Guided me to the cloister. Think, my son, On the great tsars; who loftier than they? God only. Who dares thwart them? None. What then? Often the golden crown became to them A burden; for a cowl they bartered it. The tsar Ivan sought in monastic toil Tranquility; his palace, filled erewhile With haughty minions, grew to all appearance A monastery; the very rakehells seemed Obedient monks, the terrible tsar appeared A pious abbot. Here, in this very cell (At that time Cyril, the much suffering, A righteous man, dwelt in it; even me God then made comprehend the nothingness Of worldly vanities), here I beheld, Weary of angry thoughts and executions, The tsar; among us, meditative, quiet Here sat the Terrible; we motionless Stood in his presence, while he talked with us In tranquil tones. Thus spake he to the abbot And all the brothers: "My fathers, soon will come The longed-for day; here shall

Boris Godunov: A Drama in Verse

I stand before you, Hungering for salvation; Nicodemus, Thou Sergius, Cyril thou, will all accept My spiritual vow; to you I soon shall come Accurst in sin, here the clean habit take, Prostrate, most holy father, at thy feet. " So spake the sovereign lord, and from his lips Sweetly the accents flowed. He wept; and we With tears prayed God to send His love and peace Upon his suffering and stormy soul. — What of his son Feodor? On the throne He sighed to lead the life of calm devotion. The royal chambers to a cell of prayer He turned, wherein the heavy cares of state Vexed not his holy soul. God grew to love The tsar's humility; in his good days Russia was blest with glory undisturbed, And in the hour of his decease was wrought A miracle unheard of; at his bedside, Seen by the tsar alone, appeared a being Exceeding bright, with whom Feodor 'gan To commune, calling him great Patriarch; — And all around him were possessed with fear, Musing upon the vision sent from Heaven, Since at that time the Patriarch was not present In church before the tsar. And when he died The palace was with holy fragrance filled. And like the sun his countenance outshone. Never again shall we see such a tsar. — O, horrible, appalling woe! We have sinned, We have angered God; we have chosen for our ruler A tsar's assassin.

GREGORY. Honoured father, long Have I desired to ask thee of the death Of young Dimitry, the tsarevich; thou, 'Tis said, wast then at Uglich.

PIMEN. Ay, my son, I well remember. God it was who led me To witness that ill deed, that bloody sin. I at that time was sent to distant Uglich Upon some mission. I arrived at night. Next morning, at the hour of holy mass, I heard upon a sudden a bell toll; 'Twas the alarm bell. Then a cry, an uproar; Men rushing to the court of the tsaritsa. Thither I haste, and there had flocked already All Uglich. There I see the young tsarevich Lie slaughtered: the queen mother in a swoon Bowed over him, his nurse in her despair Wailing; and then the maddened people drag The godless, treacherous nurse away. Appears Suddenly in their midst, wild, pale with rage, Judas Bityagovsky. "There, there's the villain! " Shout on all sides the crowd, and in a trice He was no more. Straightway the people rushed On the three fleeing murderers; they seized The hiding miscreants and led them up To the child's corpse yet warm; when lo! A marvel— The dead child all at once began to tremble! "Confess! " the people thundered; and in terror Beneath the axe the villains did confess— And named Boris.

GREGORY. How many summers lived The murdered boy?

PIMEN. Seven summers; he would now (Since then have passed ten years—nay, more—twelve years) He would have been of equal age to thee, And would have reigned; but God deemed otherwise. This is the lamentable tale wherewith My chronicle doth end; since then I little Have dipped in worldly business. Brother Gregory, Thou hast illumed thy mind by earnest study; To thee I hand my task. In hours exempt From the soul's exercise, do thou record, Not subtly reasoning, all things whereto Thou shalt in life be witness; war and peace, The sway of kings, the holy miracles Of saints, all prophecies and heavenly signs; — For me 'tis time to rest and quench my lamp. — But hark! The matin bell. Bless, Lord, Thy servants! Give me my crutch.

(Exit.)

GREGORY. Boris, Boris, before thee All tremble; none dares even to remind thee Of what befell the hapless child; meanwhile Here in dark cell a hermit doth indite Thy stern denunciation. Thou wilt not Escape the judgment even of this world, As thou wilt not escape the doom of God.

Boris Godunov: A Drama in Verse

FENCE OF THE MONASTERY*

*This scene was omitted by Pushkin from the published version of the play.

GREGORY and a Wicked Monk

GREGORY. O, what a weariness is our poor life, What misery! Day comes, day goes, and ever Is seen, is heard one thing alone; one sees Only black cassocks, only hears the bell. Yawning by day you wander, wander, nothing To do; you doze; the whole night long till daylight The poor monk lies awake; and when in sleep You lose yourself, black dreams disturb the soul; Glad that they sound the bell, that with a crutch They rouse you. No, I will not suffer it! I cannot! Through this fence I'll flee! The world Is great; my path is on the highways never Thou'lt hear of me again.

MONK. Truly your life Is but a sorry one, ye dissolute, Wicked young monks!

GREGORY. Would that the Khan again Would come upon us, or Lithuania rise Once more in insurrection. Good! I would then Cross swords with them! Or what if the tsarevich Should suddenly arise from out the grave, Should cry, "Where are ye, children, faithful servants? Help me against Boris, against my murderer! Seize my foe, lead him to me! "

MONK. Enough, my friend, Of empty babble. We cannot raise the dead. No, clearly it was fated otherwise For the tsarevich— But hearken; if you wish To do a thing, then do it.

GREGORY. What to do?

MONK. If I were young as thou, if these grey hairs Had not already streaked my beard— Dost take me?

GREGORY. Not I.

MONK. Hearken; our folk are dull of brain, Easy of faith, and glad to be amazed By miracles and novelties. The boyars Remember Godunov as erst he was, Peer to themselves; and even now the race

Of the old Varyags is loved by all. Thy years Match those of the tsarevich. If thou hast Cunning and hardihood— Dost take me now?

GREGORY. I take thee.

MONK. Well, what say'st thou?

GREGORY. 'Tis resolved. I am Dimitry, I tsarevich!

MONK. Give me Thy hand, my bold young friend. Thou shalt be tsar!

PALACE OF THE PATRIARCH

PATRIARCH, ABBOT of the Chudov Monastery

PATRIARCH. And he has run away, Father Abbot?

ABBOT. He has run away, holy sovereign, now three days ago.

PATRIARCH. Accursed rascal! What is his origin?

ABBOT. Of the family of the Otrepievs, of the lower nobility of Galicia; in his youth he took the tonsure, no one knows where, lived at Suzdal, in the Ephimievsky monastery, departed from there, wandered to various convents, finally arrived at my Chudov fraternity; but I, seeing that he was still young and inexperienced, entrusted him at the outset to Father Pimen, an old man, kind and humble. And he was very learned, read our chronicle, composed canons for the holy brethren; but, to be sure, instruction was not given to him from the Lord God—

PATRIARCH. Ah, those learned fellows! What a thing to say, "I shall be tsar in Moscow. " Ah, he is a vessel of the devil! However, it is no use even to report to the tsar about this; why disquiet our father sovereign? It will be enough to give information about his flight to the Secretary Smirnov or the Secretary Ephimiev. What a heresy: "I shall be tsar in Moscow! "... Catch, catch the fawning villain, and send him to Solovetsky to perpetual penance. But this—is it not heresy, Father Abbot?

ABBOT. Heresy, holy Patriarch; downright heresy.

Boris Godunov: A Drama in Verse

PALACE OF THE TSAR

Two Attendants

1ST ATTENDANT. Where is the sovereign?

2ND ATTENDANT. In his bed-chamber, Where he is closeted with some magician.

1ST ATTENDANT. Ay; that's the kind of intercourse he loves; Sorcerers, fortune-tellers, necromancers. Ever he seeks to dip into the future, Just like some pretty girl. Fain would I know What 'tis he would foretell.

2ND ATTENDANT. Well, here he comes. Will it please you question him?

1ST ATTENDANT. How grim he looks!

(Exeunt.)

TSAR. (Enters.) I have attained the highest power. Six years Already have I reigned in peace; but joy Dwells not within my soul. Even so in youth We greedily desire the joys of love, But only quell the hunger of the heart With momentary possession. We grow cold, Grow weary and oppressed! In vain the wizards Promise me length of days, days of dominion Immune from treachery—not power, not life Gladden me; I forebode the wrath of Heaven And woe. For me no happiness. I thought To satisfy my people in contentment, In glory, gain their love by generous gifts, But I have put away that empty hope; The power that lives is hateful to the mob, — Only the dead they love. We are but fools When our heart vibrates to the people's groans And passionate wailing. Lately on our land God sent a famine; perishing in torments The people uttered moan. The granaries I made them free of, scattered gold among them, Found labour for them; furious for my pains They cursed me! Next, a fire consumed their homes; I built for them new dwellings; then forsooth They blamed me for the fire! Such is the mob, Such is its judgment! Seek its love, indeed! I thought within my family to find Solace; I thought to make my daughter happy By wedlock. Like a tempest Death took off Her bridegroom—and at once a stealthy rumour Pronounced me guilty of my daughter's grief— Me, me, the hapless father! Whoso dies, I am the secret murderer of all; I hastened Feodor's end, 'twas I that poisoned My sister-queen, the lowly nun— all I! Ah! Now I feel it; naught can give us peace Mid worldly cares, nothing save only conscience! Healthy she triumphs over wickedness, Over dark slander; but if in her be found A single casual stain, then misery. With what a deadly sore my soul doth smart; My heart, with venom filled, doth like a hammer Beat in mine ears reproach; all things revolt me, And my head whirls, and in my eyes are children Dripping with blood; and gladly would I flee, But nowhere can find refuge—horrible! Pitiful he whose conscience is unclean!

Boris Godunov: A Drama in Verse

TAVERN ON THE LITHUANIAN FRONTIER

MISSAIL and VARLAAM, wandering friars; GREGORY in secular attire; HOSTESS

HOSTESS. With what shall I regale you, my reverend honoured guests?

VARLAAM. With what God sends, little hostess. Have you no wine?

HOSTESS. As if I had not, my fathers! I will bring it at once. (Exit.)

MISSAIL. Why so glum, comrade? Here is that very Lithuanian frontier which you so wished to reach.

GREGORY. Until I shall be in Lithuania, till then I shall not Be content.

VARLAAM. What is it that makes you so fond of Lithuania! Here are we, Father Missail and I, a sinner, when we fled from the monastery, then we cared for nothing. Was it Lithuania, was it Russia, was it fiddle, was it dulcimer? All the same for us, if only there was wine. That's the main thing!

MISSAIL. Well said, Father Varlaam.

HOSTESS. (Enters.) There you are, my fathers. Drink to your health.

MISSAIL. Thanks, my good friend. God bless thee. (The monks drink. Varlaam trolls a ditty: "Thou passest by, my dear, " etc.) (To GREGORY) Why don't you join in the song? Not even join in the song?

GREGORY. I don't wish to.

MISSAIL. Everyone to his liking—

VARLAAM. But a tipsy man's in Heaven. * Father Missail! We will drink a glass to our hostess. (Sings: "Where the brave lad in durance," etc.) Still, Father Missail, when I am drinking, then I don't like sober men; tipsiness is one thing—but pride quite another. If you want to live as we do, you are welcome. No? —then take yourself off, away with you; a mountebank is no companion for a priest.

[*The Russian text has here a play on the words which cannot be satisfactorily rendered into English.]

GREGORY. Drink, and keep your thoughts to yourself, * Father Varlaam! You see, I too sometimes know how to make puns.

[*The Russian text has here a play on the words which cannot be satisfactorily rendered into English.]

VARLAAM. But why should I keep my thoughts to myself?

MISSAIL. Let him alone, Father Varlaam.

VARLAAM. But what sort of a fasting man is he? Of his own accord he attached himself as a companion to us; no one knows who he is, no one knows whence he comes— and yet he gives himself grand airs; perhaps he has a close acquaintance with the pillory. (Drinks and sings: "A young monk took the tonsure, " etc.)

GREGORY. (To HOSTESS.) Whither leads this road?

HOSTESS. To Lithuania, my dear, to the Luyov mountains.

GREGORY. And is it far to the Luyov mountains?

HOSTESS. Not far; you might get there by evening, but for the tsar's frontier barriers, and the captains of the guard.

GREGORY. What say you? Barriers! What means this?

HOSTESS. Someone has escaped from Moscow, and orders have been given to detain and search everyone.

GREGORY. (Aside.) Here's a pretty mess!

VARLAAM. Hallo, comrade! You've been making up to mine hostess. To be sure you don't want vodka, but you want a young woman. All right, brother, all right! Everyone has his own ways, and Father Missail and I have only one thing which we care for—we drink to the bottom, we drink; turn it upside down, and knock at the bottom.

MISSAIL. Well said, Father Varlaam.

GREGORY. (To Hostess.) Whom do they want? Who escaped from Moscow?

HOSTESS. God knows; a thief perhaps, a robber. But here even good folk are worried now. And what will come of it? Nothing. They will not catch the old devil; as if there were no other road into Lithuania than the highway! Just turn to the left from here, then by the pinewood or by the footpath as far as the chapel on the Chekansky brook, and then straight across the marsh to Khlopin, and thence to Zakhariev, and then any child will guide you to the Luyov mountains. The only good of these inspectors is to worry passers-by and rob us poor folk. (A noise is heard.) What's that? Ah, there they are, curse them! They are going their rounds.

GREGORY. Hostess! Is there another room in the cottage?

HOSTESS. No, my dear; I should be glad myself to hide. But they are only pretending to go their rounds; but give them wine and bread, and Heaven knows what— May perdition take them, the accursed ones! May—

(Enter OFFICERS.)

OFFICERS. Good health to you, mine hostess!

HOSTESS. You are kindly welcome, dear guests.

AN OFFICER. (To another.) Ha, there's drinking going on here; we shall get something here. (To the Monks.) Who are you?

VARLAAM. We—are two old clerics, humble monks; we are going from village to village, and collecting Christian alms for the monastery.

OFFICER. (To GREGORY.) And thou?

MISSAIL. Our comrade.

Boris Godunov: A Drama in Verse

GREGORY. A layman from the suburb; I have conducted the old men as far as the frontier; from here I am going to my own home.

MISSAIL. So you have changed your mind?

GREGORY. (Sotto voce.) Be silent.

OFFICER. Hostess, bring some more wine, and we will drink here a little and talk a little with these old men.

2ND OFFICER. (Sotto voce.) Yon lad, it appears, is poor; there's nothing to be got out of him; on the other hand the old men—

1ST OFFICER. Be silent; we shall come to them presently. —Well, my fathers, how are you getting on?

VARLAAM. Badly, my sons, badly! The Christians have now turned stingy; they love their money; they hide their money. They give little to God. The people of the world have become great sinners. They have all devoted themselves to commerce, to earthly cares; they think of worldly wealth, not of the salvation of the soul. You walk and walk; you beg and beg; sometimes in three days begging will not bring you three half-pence. What a sin! A week goes by; another week; you look into your bag, and there is so little in it that you are ashamed to show yourself at the monastery. What are you to do? From very sorrow you drink away what is left; a real calamity! Ah, it is bad! It seems our last days have come—

HOSTESS. (Weeps.) God pardon and save you! (During the course of VARLAAM'S speech the 1st OFFICER watches MISSAIL significantly.)

1ST OFFICER. Alexis! Have you the tsar's edict with you?

2ND OFFICER. I have it.

1ST OFFICER. Give it here.

MISSAIL. Why do you look at me so fixedly?

1ST OFFICER. This is why; from Moscow there has fled a certain wicked heretic—Grishka Otrepiev. Have you heard this?

MISSAIL. I have not heard it.

OFFICER. Not heard it? Very good. And the tsar has ordered to arrest and hang the fugitive heretic. Do you know this?

MISSAIL. I do not know it.

OFFICER. (To VARLAAM.) Do you know how to read?

VARLAAM. In my youth I knew how, but I have forgotten.

OFFICER. (To MISSAIL.) And thou?

MISSAIL. God has not made me wise.

OFFICER. So then here's the tsar's edict.

MISSAIL. What do I want it for?

OFFICER. It seems to me that this fugitive heretic, thief, swindler, is—thou.

MISSAIL. I? Good gracious! What are you talking about?

OFFICER. Stay! Hold the doors. Then we shall soon get at the truth.

HOSTESS. O the cursed tormentors! Not to leave even the old man in peace!

OFFICER. Which of you here is a scholar?

GREGORY. (Comes forward.) I am a scholar!

OFFICER. Oh, indeed! And from whom did you learn?

GREGORY. From our sacristan.

OFFICER (Gives him the edict.) Read it aloud.

GREGORY. (Reads.) "An unworthy monk of the Monastery Of Chudov, Gregory, of the family of Otrepiev, has fallen into heresy, taught by the devil, and has dared to vex the holy brotherhood by all kinds of iniquities and acts of lawlessness. And, according to information, it has been shown that he, the accursed Grishka, has fled to the Lithuanian frontier."

OFFICER. (To MISSAIL.) How can it be anyone but you?

GREGORY. "And the tsar has commanded to arrest him—"

OFFICER. And to hang!

GREGORY. It does not say here "to hang."

OFFICER. Thou liest. What is meant is not always put into writing. Read: to arrest and to hang.

GREGORY. "And to hang. And the age of the thief Grishka" (looking at VARLAAM) "about fifty, and his height medium; he has a bald head, grey beard, fat belly."

(All glance at VARLAAM.)

1ST OFFICER, My lads! Here is Grishka! Hold him! Bind him! I never thought to catch him so quickly.

VARLAAM. (Snatching the paper.) Hands off, my lads! What sort of a Grishka am I? What! Fifty years old, grey beard, fat belly! No, brother. You're too young to play off tricks on me. I have not read for a long time and I make it out badly, but I shall manage to make it out, as it's a hanging matter. (Spells it out.) "And his age twenty." Why, brother, where does it say fifty? — Do you see—twenty?

2ND OFFICER. Yes, I remember, twenty; even so it was told us.

1ST OFFICER. (To GREGORY.) Then, evidently, you like a joke, brother.

(During the reading GREGORY stands with downcast head, and his hand in his breast.)

VARLAAM. (Continues.) "And in stature he is small, chest broad, one arm shorter than the other, blue eyes, red hair, a wart on his cheek, another on his forehead." Then is it not you, my friend?

(GREGORY suddenly draws a dagger; all give way before him; he dashes through the window.)

OFFICERS. Hold him! Hold him!

(All run out in disorder.)

MOSCOW. SHUISKY'S HOUSE

SHUISKY. A number of Guests. Supper

SHUISKY. More wine! Now, my dear guests.

(He rises; all rise after him.)

The final draught! Read the prayer, boy.

Boy. Lord of the heavens, Who art Eternally and everywhere, accept The prayer of us Thy servants. For our monarch, By Thee appointed, for our pious tsar, Of all good Christians autocrat, we pray. Preserve him in the palace, on the field Of battle, on his nightly couch; grant to him Victory o'er his foes; from sea to sea May he be glorified; may all his house Blossom with health, and may its precious branches O'ershadow all the earth; to us, his slaves, May he, as heretofore, be generous. Gracious, long-suffering, and may the founts Of his unfailing wisdom flow upon us; Raising the royal cup, Lord of the heavens, For this we pray.

SHUISKY. (Drinks.) Long live our mighty sovereign! Farewell, dear guests. I thank you that ye scorned not My bread and salt. Farewell; good-night.

(Exeunt Guests: he conducts them to the door.)

PUSHKIN. Hardly could they tear themselves away; indeed, Prince Vassily Ivanovitch, I began to think that we should not succeed in getting any private talk.

SHUISKY. (To the Servants.) You there, why do you stand Gaping? Always eavesdropping on gentlemen! Clear the table, and then be off.

(Exeunt Servants.)

What is it, Athanasius Mikailovitch?

PUSHKIN. Such a wondrous thing! A message was sent here to me today From Cracow by my nephew Gabriel Pushkin.

SHUISKY. Well?

PUSHKIN. 'Tis strange news my nephew writes. The son Of the Terrible— But stay—

(Goes to the door and examines it.)

The royal boy, Who murdered was by order of Boris—

SHUISKY. But these are no new tidings.

PUSHKIN. Wait a little; Dimitry lives.

SHUISKY. So that's it! News indeed! Dimitry living! —Really marvelous! And is that all?

PUSHKIN. Pray listen to the end; Whoe'er he be, whether he be Dimitry Rescued, or else some spirit in his shape, Some daring rogue, some insolent pretender, In any case Dimitry has appeared.

SHUISKY. It cannot be.

PUSHKIN. Pushkin himself beheld him When first he reached the court, and through the ranks Of Lithuanian gentlemen went straight Into the secret chamber of the king.

SHUISKY. What kind of man? Whence comes he?

PUSHKIN. No one knows. 'Tis known that he was Vishnevetsky's servant; That to a ghostly father on a bed Of sickness he disclosed himself; possessed Of this strange secret, his proud master nursed him, >From his sick bed upraised him, and straightway Took him to Sigismund.

SHUISKY. And what say men Of this bold fellow?

PUSHKIN. 'Tis said that he is wise, Affable, cunning, popular with all men. He has bewitched the fugitives from Moscow, The Catholic priests see eye to eye with him. The King caresses him, and, it is said, Has promised help.

SHUISKY. All this is such a medley That my head whirls. Brother, beyond all doubt This man is a pretender, but the danger Is, I confess, not slight. This is grave news! And if it reach the people, then there'll be A mighty tempest.

PUSHKIN. Such a storm that hardly Will Tsar Boris contrive to keep the crown Upon his clever head; and losing it Will get but his deserts! He governs us As did the tsar Ivan of evil memory. What profits it that public executions Have ceased, that we no longer sing in public Hymns to Christ Jesus on the field of blood; That we no more are burnt in public places, Or that the tsar no longer with his sceptre Rakes in the ashes? Is there any safety In our poor life? Each day disgrace awaits us; The dungeon or Siberia, cowl or fetters, And then in some deaf nook a starving death, Or else the halter. Where are the most renowned Of all our houses, where the Sitsky princes, Where are the Shestunovs, where the Romanovs, Hope of our fatherland? Imprisoned, tortured, In exile. Do but wait, and a like fate Will soon be thine. Think of it! Here at home, Just as in Lithuania, we're beset By treacherous slaves—and tongues are ever ready For base betrayal, thieves bribed by the State. We hang upon the word of the first servant Whom we may please to punish. Then he bethought him To take from us our privilege of hiring Our serfs at will; we are no longer masters Of our own lands. Presume not to dismiss An idler. Willy nilly, thou must feed him! Presume not to outbid a man in hiring A labourer, or you will find yourself In the Court's clutches. —Was such an evil heard of Even under tsar Ivan? And are the people The better off? Ask them. Let the pretender But promise them the old free right of transfer, Then there'll be sport.

SHUISKY. Thou'rt right; but be advised; Of this, of all things, for a time we'll speak No word.

PUSHKIN. Assuredly, keep thine own counsel. Thou art—a person of discretion; always I am glad to commune with thee; and if aught At any time disturbs me, I endure not To keep it from thee; and, truth to tell, thy mead And velvet ale today have so untied My tongue... Farewell then, prince.

SHUISKY. Brother, farewell. Farewell, my brother, till we meet again.
(He escorts PUSHKIN out.)

Boris Godunov: A Drama in Verse

PALACE OF THE TSAR

The TSAREVICH is drawing a map. The TSAREVNA. The NURSE of the Tsarevna

KSENIA. (Kisses a portrait.) My dear bridegroom, comely son of a king, not to me wast thou given, not to thy affianced bride, but to a dark sepulchre in a strange land; never shall I take comfort, ever shall I weep for thee.

NURSE. Eh, tsarevna! A maiden weeps as the dew falls; the sun will rise, will dry the dew. Thou wilt have another bridegroom—and handsome and affable. My charming child, thou wilt learn to love him, thou wilt forget Ivan the king's son.

KSENIA. Nay, nurse, I will be true to him even in death.

(Boris enters.)

TSAR. What, Ksenia? What, my sweet one? In thy girlhood Already a woe-stricken widow, ever Bewailing thy dead bridegroom! Fate forbade me To be the author of thy bliss. Perchance I angered Heaven; it was not mine to compass Thy happiness. Innocent one, for what Art thou a sufferer? And thou, my son, With what art thou employed? What's this?

FEODOR. A chart Of all the land of Muscovy; our tsardom From end to end. Here you see; there is Moscow, There Novgorod, there Astrakhan. Here lies The sea, here the dense forest tract of Perm, And here Siberia.

TSAR. And what is this Which makes a winding pattern here?

FEODOR. That is The Volga.

TSAR. Very good! Here's the sweet fruit Of learning. One can view as from the clouds Our whole dominion at a glance; its frontiers, Its towns, its rivers. Learn, my son; 'tis science Which gives to us an abstract of the events Of our swift-flowing life. Some day, perchance Soon, all the lands which thou so cunningly Today hast drawn on paper, all will come Under thy hand. Learn, therefore; and more smoothly, More clearly wilt thou take, my son, upon thee The cares of state.

(SEMYON Godunov enters.)

But there comes Godunov Bringing reports to me. (To KSENIA.) Go to thy chamber Dearest; farewell, my child; God comfort thee.

(Exeunt KSENIA and NURSE.)

What news hast thou for me, Semyon Nikitich?

SEMYON G. Today at dawn the butler of Prince Shuisky And Pushkin's servant brought me information.

TSAR. Well?

SEMYON G. In the first place Pushkin's man deposed That yestermorn came to his house from Cracow A courier, who within an hour was sent Without a letter back.

TSAR. Arrest the courier.

SEMYON G. Some are already sent to overtake him.

TSAR. And what of Shuisky?

SEMYON G. Last night he entertained His friends; the Buturlins, both Miloslavskys, And Saltikov, with Pushkin and some others. They parted late. Pushkin alone remained Closeted with his host and talked with him A long time more.

TSAR. For Shuisky send forthwith.

SEMYON G. Sire, he is here already.

TSAR. Call him hither.

(Exit SEMYON Godunov.)

Dealings with Lithuania? What means this? I like not the seditious race of Pushkins, Nor must I trust in Shuisky, obsequious, But bold and wily —

Boris Godunov: A Drama in Verse

(Enter SHUISKY.)

Prince, I must speak with thee. But thou thyself, it seems, hast business with me, And I would listen first to thee.

SHUISKY. Yea, sire; It is my duty to convey to thee Grave news.

TSAR. I listen.

SHUISKY. (Sotto voce, pointing to FEODOR.) But, sire—

TSAR. The tsarevich May learn whate'er Prince Shuisky knoweth. Speak.

SHUISKY. My liege, from Lithuania there have come Tidings to us—

TSAR. Are they not those same tidings Which yestereve a courier bore to Pushkin?

SHUISKY. Nothing is hidden from him! —Sire, I thought Thou knew'st not yet this secret.

TSAR. Let not that Trouble thee, prince; I fain would scrutinise Thy information; else we shall not learn The actual truth.

SHUISKY. I know this only, Sire; In Cracow a pretender hath appeared; The king and nobles back him.

TSAR. What say they? And who is this pretender?

SHUISKY. I know not.

TSAR. But wherein is he dangerous?

SHUISKY. Verily Thy state, my liege, is firm; by graciousness, Zeal, bounty, thou hast won the filial love Of all thy slaves; but thou thyself dost know The mob is thoughtless, changeable, rebellious, Credulous, lightly given to vain hope, Obedient to each momentary impulse, To truth deaf and indifferent; it feedeth On fables; shameless boldness pleaseth it. So, if this unknown vagabond should cross The Lithuanian border, Dimitry's name Raised from the grave will gain him a whole crowd Of fools.

TSAR. Dimitry's? —What? —That child's? —Dimitry's? Withdraw, tsarevich.

SHUISKY. He flushed; there'll be a storm!

FEODOR. Suffer me, Sire—

TSAR. Impossible, my son; Go, go!

(Exit FEODOR.)

Dimitry's name!

SHUISKY. Then he knew nothing.

TSAR. Listen: take steps this very hour that Russia Be fenced by barriers from Lithuania; That not a single soul pass o'er the border, That not a hare run o'er to us from Poland, Nor crow fly here from Cracow. Away!

SHUISKY. I go.

TSAR. Stay! —Is it not a fact that this report Is artfully concocted? Hast ever heard That dead men have arisen from their graves To question tsars, legitimate tsars, appointed, Chosen by the voice of all the people, crowned By the great Patriarch? Is't not laughable? Eh? What? Why laugh'st thou not thereat?

SHUISKY. I, Sire?

TSAR. Hark, Prince Vassily; when first I learned this child Had been—this child had somehow lost its life, 'Twas thou I sent to search the matter out. Now by the Cross and God I do adjure thee, Declare to me the truth upon thy conscience; Didst recognise the slaughtered boy; was't not A substitute? Reply.

SHUISKY. I swear to thee—

TSAR. Nay, Shuisky, swear not, but reply; was it Indeed Dimitry?

SHUISKY. He.

TSAR. Consider, prince. I promise clemency; I will not punish With vain disgrace a lie that's past. But if Thou now beguile me, then by my son's head I swear—an evil fate shall overtake thee, Requital such that Tsar Ivan Vasilievich Shall shudder in his grave with horror of it.

SHUISKY. In punishment no terror lies; the terror Doth lie in thy disfavour; in thy presence Dare I use cunning? Could I deceive myself So blindly as not recognise Dimitry? Three days in the cathedral did I visit His corpse, escorted thither by all Uglich. Around him thirteen bodies lay of those Slain by the people, and on them corruption Already had set in perceptibly. But lo! The childish face of the tsarevich Was bright and fresh and quiet as if asleep; The deep gash had congealed not, nor the lines Of his face even altered. No, my liege, There is no doubt; Dimitry sleeps in the grave.

TSAR. Enough, withdraw.

(Exit SHUISKY.)

I choke! —let me get my breath! I felt it; all my blood surged to my face, And heavily fell back. —So that is why For thirteen years together I have dreamed Ever about the murdered child. Yes, yes— 'Tis that! —now I perceive. But who is he, My terrible antagonist? Who is it Opposeth me? An empty name, a shadow. Can it be a shade shall tear from me the purple, A sound deprive my children of succession? Fool that I was! Of what was I afraid? Blow on this phantom—and it is no more. So, I am fast resolved; I'll show no sign Of fear, but nothing must be held in scorn. Ah! Heavy art thou, crown of Monomakh!

CRACOW. HOUSE OF VISHNEVETSKY

The PRETENDER and a CATHOLIC PRIEST

PRETENDER. Nay, father, there will be no trouble. I know The spirit of my people; piety Does not run wild in them, their tsar's example To them is sacred. Furthermore, the people Are always tolerant. I warrant you, Before two years my people all, and all The Eastern Church, will recognise the power Of Peter's Vicar.

PRIEST. May Saint Ignatius aid thee When other times shall come. Meanwhile, tsarevich, Hide in thy soul the seed of heavenly blessing; Religious duty bids us oft dissemble Before the blabbing world; the people judge Thy words, thy deeds; God only sees thy motives.

PRETENDER. Amen. Who's there?

(Enter a Servant.)

Say that we will receive them.

(The doors are opened; a crowd of Russians and Poles enters.)

Comrades! Tomorrow we depart from Cracow. Mnishek, with thee for three days in Sambor I'll stay. I know thy hospitable castle Both shines in splendid stateliness, and glories In its young mistress; There I hope to see Charming Marina. And ye, my friends, ye, Russia And Lithuania, ye who have upraised Fraternal banners against a common foe, Against mine enemy, yon crafty villain. Ye sons of Slavs, speedily will I lead Your dread battalions to the longed-for conflict. But soft! Methinks among you I descry New faces.

GABRIEL P. They have come to beg for sword And service with your Grace.

PRETENDER. Welcome, my lads. You are friends to me. But tell me, Pushkin, who Is this fine fellow?

PUSHKIN. Prince Kurbsky.

PRETENDER. (To KURBSKY.) A famous name! Art kinsman to the hero of Kazan?

KURBSKY. His son.

PRETENDER. Liveth he still?

KURBSKY. Nay, he is dead.

PRETENDER. A noble soul! A man of war and counsel. But from the time when he appeared beneath The ancient town Olgin with the Lithuanians, Hardy avenger of his injuries, Rumour hath held her tongue concerning him.

KURBSKY. My father led the remnant of his life On lands bestowed upon him by Batory; There, in Volhynia, solitary and quiet, Sought consolation for himself in studies; But peaceful labour did not comfort him; He ne'er forgot the home of his young days, And to the end pined for it.

PRETENDER. Hapless chieftain! How brightly shone the dawn of his resounding And stormy life! Glad am I, noble knight, That now his blood is reconciled in thee To his fatherland. The faults of fathers must not Be called to mind. Peace to their grave. Approach; Give me thy hand! Is it not strange? —the son Of Kurbsky to the throne is leading—whom? Whom but Ivan's own son? —All favours me; People and fate alike. —Say, who art thou?

A POLE. Sobansky, a free noble.

PRETENDER. Praise and honour Attend thee, child of liberty. Give him A third of his full pay beforehand. —Who Are these? On them I recognise the dress Of my own country. These are ours.

KRUSHCHOV. (Bows low.) Yea, Sire, Our father; we are thralls of thine, devoted And persecuted; we have fled from Moscow, Disgraced, to thee our tsar, and for thy sake Are ready to lay down our lives; our corpses Shall be for thee steps to the royal throne.

PRETENDER. Take heart, innocent sufferers. Only let me Reach Moscow, and, once there, Boris shall settle Some scores with me and you. What news of Moscow?

KRUSHCHOV. As yet all there is quiet. But already The folk have got to know that the tsarevich Was saved; already everywhere is read Thy proclamation. All are waiting for thee. Not long ago Boris

Boris Godunov: A Drama in Verse

sent two boyars To execution merely because in secret They drank thy health.

PRETENDER. O hapless, good boyars! But blood for blood! And woe to Godunov! What do they say of him?

KRUSHCHOV. He has withdrawn Into his gloomy palace. He is grim And sombre. Executions loom ahead. But sickness gnaws him. Hardly hath he strength To drag himself along, and—it is thought— His last hour is already not far off.

PRETENDER. A speedy death I wish him, as becomes A great-souled foe to wish. If not, then woe To the miscreant! —And whom doth he intend To name as his successor?

KRUSHCHOV. He shows not His purposes, but it would seem he destines Feodor, his young son, to be our tsar.

PRETENDER. His reckonings, maybe, will yet prove wrong. Who art thou?

KARELA. A Cossack; from the Don I am sent To thee, from the free troops, from the brave hetmen From upper and lower regions of the Cossacks, To look upon thy bright and royal eyes, And tender thee their homage.

PRETENDER. Well I knew The men of Don; I doubted not to see The Cossack hetmen in my ranks. We thank Our army of the Don. Today, we know, The Cossacks are unjustly persecuted, Oppressed; but if God grant us to ascend The throne of our forefathers, then as of yore We'll gratify the free and faithful Don.

POET. (Approaches. bowing low, and taking Gregory by the hem of his caftan.) Great prince, illustrious offspring of a king!

PRETENDER. What wouldst thou?

POET. Condescendingly accept This poor fruit of my earnest toil.

PRETENDER. What see I? Verses in Latin! Blest a hundredfold The tie of sword and lyre; the selfsame laurel Binds them in friendship. I was born beneath A northern sky, but yet the Latin muse To me is a familiar voice; I love The blossoms of Parnassus, I believe The

Boris Godunov: A Drama in Verse

prophecies of singers. Not in vain The ecstasy boils in their flaming breast; Action is hallowed, being glorified Beforehand by the poets! Approach, my friend. In memory of me accept this gift.

(Gives him a ring.)

When fate fulfils for me her covenant, When I assume the crown of my forefathers, I hope again to hear the measured tones Of thy sweet voice, and thy inspired lay. Musa gloriam Coronat, gloriaque musam. And so, friends, till tomorrow, au revoir.

ALL. Forward! Long live Dimitry! Forward, forward! Long live Dimitry, the great prince of Moscow!

CASTLE OF THE GOVERNOR

MNISHEK IN SAMBOR

Dressing-Room of Marina

MARINA, ROUZYA (dressing her), Serving-Women

MARINA. (Before a mirror.) Now then, is it ready? Cannot you make haste?

ROUZYA. I pray you first to make the difficult choice; Will you the necklace wear of pearls, or else The emerald half-moon?

MARINA. My diamond crown.

ROUZYA. Splendid! Do you remember that you wore it When to the palace you were pleased to go? They say that at the ball your gracious highness Shone like the sun; men sighed, fair ladies whispered— 'Twas then that for the first time young Khotkevich Beheld you, he who after shot himself. And whosoever looked on you, they say That instant fell in love.

MARINA. Can't you be quicker?

ROUZYA. At once. Today your father counts upon you. 'Twas not for naught the young tsarevich saw you; He could not hide his rapture; wounded he is Already; so it only needs to deal him A resolute blow, and instantly, my lady, He'll be in love with you. 'Tis now a month Since, quitting Cracow, heedless of the war And throne of Moscow, he has feasted here, Your guest, enraging Poles alike and Russians. Heavens! Shall I ever live to see the day? — Say, you will not, when to his capital Dimitry leads the queen of Moscow, say You'll not forsake me?

MARINA. Dost thou truly think I shall be queen?

ROUZYA. Who, if not you? Who here Dares to compare in beauty with my mistress? The race of Mnishek never yet has yielded To any. In intellect you are beyond All praise. —Happy the suitor whom your glance Honours with its regard, who wins your heart— Whoe'er he be, be he our king, the dauphin Of France, or even this our poor tsarevich God knows who, God knows whence!

MARINA. The very son Of the tsar, and so confessed by the whole world.

ROUZYA. And yet last winter he was but a servant In the house of Vishnevetsky.

MARINA. He was hiding.

ROUZYA. I do not question it: but still do you know What people say about him? That perhaps He is a deacon run away from Moscow, In his own district a notorious rogue.

MARINA. What nonsense!

ROUZYA. O, I do not credit it! I only say he ought to bless his fate That you have so preferred him to the others.

WAITING-WOMAN. (Runs in.) The guests have come already.

MARINA. There you see; You're ready to chatter silliness till daybreak. Meanwhile I am not dressed—

ROUZYA. Within a moment 'Twill be quite ready.

(The Waiting-women bustle.)

MARINA. (Aside.) I must find out all.

Boris Godunov: A Drama in Verse

A SUITE OF LIGHTED ROOMS.

VISHNEVETSKY, MNISHEK

MNISHEK. With none but my Marina doth he speak, With no one else consorteth—and that business Looks dreadfully like marriage. Now confess, Didst ever think my daughter would be a queen?

VISHNEVETSKY. 'Tis wonderful. —And, Mnishek, didst thou think My servant would ascend the throne of Moscow?

MNISHEK. And what a girl, look you, is my Marina. I merely hinted to her: "Now, be careful! Let not Dimitry slip"—and lo! Already He is completely tangled in her toils.

(The band plays a Polonaise. The PRETENDER and MARINA advance as the first couple.)

MARINA. (Sotto voce to Dimitry.) Tomorrow evening at eleven, beside The fountain in the avenue of lime-trees.

(They walk off. A second couple.)

CAVALIER. What can Dimitry see in her?

DAME. How say you? She is a beauty.

CAVALIER. Yes, a marble nymph; Eyes, lips, devoid of life, without a smile.

(A fresh couple.)

DAME. He is not handsome, but his eyes are pleasing, And one can see he is of royal birth.

(A fresh couple.)

DAME. When will the army march?

CAVALIER. When the tsarevich Orders it; we are ready; but 'tis clear The lady Mnishek and Dimitry mean To keep us prisoners here.

DAME. A pleasant durance.

CAVALIER. Truly, if you...

(They walk off; the rooms become empty.)

MNISHEK. We old ones dance no longer; The sound of music lures us not; we press not Nor kiss the hands of charmers—ah! My friend, I've not forgotten the old pranks! Things now Are not what once they were, what once they were! Youth, I'll be sworn, is not so bold, nor beauty So lively; everything—confess, my friend— Has somehow become dull. So let us leave them; My comrade, let us go and find a flask Of old Hungarian overgrown with mould; Let's bid my butler open an old bottle, And in a quiet corner, tete-a-tete, Let's drain a draught, a stream as thick as fat; And while we're so engaged, let's think things over. Let us go, brother.

VISHNEVETSKY. Yes, my friend, let's go.

Boris Godunov: A Drama in Verse

NIGHT

THE GARDEN. THE FOUNTAIN

PRETENDER. (Enters.) Here is the fountain; hither will she come. I was not born a coward; I have seen Death near at hand, and face to face with death My spirit hath not blenched. A life-long dungeon Hath threatened me, I have been close pursued, And yet my spirit quailed not, and by boldness I have escaped captivity. But what Is this which now constricts my breath? What means This overpowering tremor, or this quivering Of tense desire? No, this is fear. All day I have waited for this secret meeting, pondered On all that I should say to her, how best I might enmesh Marina's haughty mind, Calling her queen of Moscow. But the hour Has come—and I remember naught, I cannot Recall the speeches I have learned by rote; Love puts imagination to confusion— But something there gleamed suddenly—a rustling; Hush—no, it was the moon's deceitful light, It was the rustling of the breeze.

MARINA. (Enters.) Tsarevich!

PRETENDER. 'Tis she. Now all the blood in me stands still.

MARINA. Dimitry! Is it thou?

PRETENDER. Bewitching voice!

(Goes to her.)

Is it thou, at last? Is it thou I see, alone With me, beneath the roof of quiet night? How slowly passed the tedious day! How slowly The glow of evening died away! How long I have waited in the gloom of night!

MARINA. The hours Are flitting fast, and time is precious to me. I did not grant a meeting here to thee To listen to a lover's tender speeches. No need of words. I well believe thou lovest; But listen; with thy stormy, doubtful fate I have resolved to join my own; but one thing, Dimitry, I require; I claim that thou Disclose to me thy secret hopes, thy plans, Even thy fears, that hand in hand with thee I may confront life boldly—not in blindness Of childlike ignorance, not as the slave And plaything of my husband's light desires, Thy speechless concubine, but as thy spouse, And worthy helpmate of the tsar of Moscow.

PRETENDER. O, if it be only for one short hour, Forget the cares and troubles of my fate! Forget 'tis the tsarevich whom thou seest Before thee. O, behold in me, Marina, A lover, by thee chosen, happy only In thy regard. O, listen to the prayers Of love! Grant me to utter all wherewith My heart is full.

MARINA. Prince, this is not the time; Thou loiterest, and meanwhile the devotion Of thine adherents cooleth. Hour by hour Danger becomes more dangerous, difficulties More difficult; already dubious rumours Are current, novelty already takes The place of novelty; and Godunov Adopts his measures.

PRETENDER. What is Godunov? Is thy sweet love, my only blessedness, Swayed by Boris? Nay, nay. Indifferently I now regard his throne, his kingly power. Thy love—without it what to me is life, And glory's glitter, and the state of Russia? On the dull steppe, in a poor mud hut, thou— Thou wilt requite me for the kingly crown; Thy love—

MARINA. For shame! Forget not, prince, thy high And sacred destiny; thy dignity Should be to thee more dear than all the joys Of life and its allurements. It thou canst not With anything compare. Not to a boy, Insanely boiling, captured by my beauty— But to the heir of Moscow's throne give I My hand in solemn wise, to the tsarevich Rescued by destiny.

PRETENDER. Torture me not, Charming Marina; say not that 'twas my rank And not myself that thou didst choose. Marina! Thou knowest not how sorely thou dost wound My heart thereby. What if—O fearful doubt! — Say, if blind destiny had not assigned me A kingly birth; if I were not indeed Son of Ivan, were not this boy, so long Forgotten by the world—say, then wouldst thou Have loved me?

MARINA. Thou art Dimitry, and aught else Thou canst not be; it is not possible For me to love another.

PRETENDER. Nay! Enough— I have no wish to share with a dead body A mistress who belongs to him; I have done With counterfeiting, and will tell the truth. Know, then, that thy Dimitry long ago Perished, was buried—and will not rise again; And dost thou wish to know what man I am? Well, I will tell thee. I am—a poor monk. Grown weary of monastic servitude, I pondered 'neath the cowl my bold design, Made ready for the world a miracle— And from my cell at last fled to the Cossacks, To their wild hovels; there I learned to handle Both steeds and swords; I showed myself to you. I called myself Dimitry, and deceived The brainless Poles. What say'st thou, proud Marina? Art thou content with my confession? Why Dost thou keep silence?

MARINA. O shame! O woe is me!

(Silence.)

PRETENDER. (Sotto voce.) O whither hath a fit of anger led me? The happiness devised with so much labour I have, perchance, destroyed for ever. Idiot, What have I done? (Aloud.) I see thou art ashamed Of love not princely; so pronounce on me The fatal word; my fate is in thy hands. Decide; I wait.

(Falls on his knees.)

MARINA. Rise, poor pretender! Think'st thou To please with genuflex on my vain heart, As if I were a weak, confiding girl? You err, my friend; prone at my feet I've seen Knights and counts nobly born; but not for this Did I reject their prayers, that a poor monk—

PRETENDER. (Rises.) Scorn not the young pretender; noble virtues May lie perchance in him, virtues well worthy Of Moscow's throne, even of thy priceless hand—

MARINA. Say of a shameful noose, insolent wretch!

PRETENDER. I am to blame; carried away by pride I have deceived God and the kings—have lied To the world; but it is not for thee, Marina, To judge me; I am guiltless before thee. No, I could not deceive thee. Thou to me Wast the one sacred being, before thee I dared not to dissemble; love alone, Love, jealous, blind, constrained me to tell all.

MARINA. What's that to boast of, idiot? Who demanded Confession of thee? If thou, a nameless vagrant Couldst wonderfully blind two nations, then At least thou shouldst have merited success, And thy bold fraud secured, by constant, deep, And lasting secrecy. Say, can I yield Myself to thee, can I, forgetting rank And maiden modesty, unite my fate With thine, when thou thyself impetuously Dost thus with such simplicity reveal Thy shame? It was from Love he blabbed to me! I marvel wherefore thou hast not from friendship Disclosed thyself ere now before my father, Or else before our king from joy, or else Before Prince Vishnevetsky from the zeal Of a devoted servant.

PRETENDER. I swear to thee That thou alone wast able to extort My heart's confession; I swear to thee that never, Nowhere, not in the feast, not in the cup Of folly, not in friendly confidence, Not 'neath the knife nor tortures of the rack, Shall my tongue give away these weighty secrets.

MARINA. Thou swearest! Then I must believe. Believe, Of course! But may I learn by what thou swearest? Is it not by the name of God, as suits The Jesuits' devout adopted son? Or by thy honour as a high-born knight? Or, maybe, by thy royal word alone As a king's son? Is it not so? Declare.

PRETENDER. (Proudly.) The phantom of the Terrible hath made me His son; from out the sepulchre hath named me Dimitry, hath stirred up the people round me, And hath consigned Boris to be my victim. I am tsarevich. Enough! 'Twere shame for me To stoop before a haughty Polish dame. Farewell for ever; the game of bloody war, The wide cares of my destiny, will smother, I hope, the pangs Of love. O, when the heat Of shameful passion is o'erspent, how then Shall I detest thee! Now I leave thee—ruin, Or else a crown, awaits my head in Russia; Whether I meet with death as fits a soldier In honourable fight, or as a miscreant Upon the public scaffold, thou shalt not Be my companion, nor shalt share with me My fate; but it may be thou shalt regret The destiny thou hast refused.

MARINA. But what If I expose beforehand thy bold fraud To all men?

PRETENDER. Dost thou think I fear thee? Think'st thou They will believe a Polish maiden more Than Russia's own tsarevich? Know, proud lady, That neither king, nor pope, nor nobles trouble Whether my words be true, whether I be Dimitry or another. What care they? But I provide a pretext for revolt And war; and this is all they need; and thee, Rebellious one, believe me, they will force To hold thy peace. Farewell.

MARINA. Tsarevich, stay! At last I hear the speech not of a boy, But of a man. It reconciles me to thee. Prince, I forget thy senseless outburst, see Again Dimitry. Listen; now is the time! Hasten; delay no more, lead on thy troops Quickly to Moscow, purge the Kremlin, take Thy seat upon the throne of Moscow; then Send me the nuptial envoy; but, God hears me, Until thy foot be planted on its steps, Until by thee Boris be overthrown, I am not one to listen to love-speeches.

PRETENDER. No—easier far to strive with Godunov. Or play false with the Jesuits of the Court, Than with a woman. Deuce take them; they're beyond My power. She twists, and coils, and crawls, slips out Of hand, she hisses, threatens, bites. Ah, serpent! Serpent! 'Twas not for nothing that I trembled. She well-nigh ruined me; but I'm resolved; At daybreak I will put my troops in motion.

Boris Godunov: A Drama in Verse

THE LITHUANIAN FRONTIER

(OCTOBER 16TH, 1604)

PRINCE KURBSKY and PRETENDER, both on horseback. Troops approach the Frontier

KURBSKY. (Galloping at their head.) There, there it is; there is the Russian frontier! Fatherland! Holy Russia! I am thine! With scorn from off my clothing now I shake The foreign dust, and greedily I drink New air; it is my native air. O father, Thy soul hath now been solaced; in the grave Thy bones, disgraced, thrill with a sudden joy! Again doth flash our old ancestral sword, This glorious sword—the dread of dark Kazan! This good sword—servant of the tsars of Moscow! Now will it revel in its feast of slaughter, Serving the master of its hopes.

PRETENDER. (Moves quietly with bowed head.) How happy Is he, how flushed with gladness and with glory His stainless soul! Brave knight, I envy thee! The son of Kurbsky, nurtured in exile, Forgetting all the wrongs borne by thy father, Redeeming his transgression in the grave, Ready art thou for the son of great Ivan To shed thy blood, to give the fatherland Its lawful tsar. Righteous art thou; thy soul Should flame with joy.

KURBSKY. And dost not thou likewise Rejoice in spirit? There lies our Russia; she Is thine, tsarevich! There thy people's hearts Are waiting for thee, there thy Moscow waits, Thy Kremlin, thy dominion.

PRETENDER. Russian blood, O Kurbsky, first must flow! Thou for the tsar Hast drawn the sword, thou art stainless; but I lead you Against your brothers; I am summoning Lithuania against Russia; I am showing To foes the longed-for way to beauteous Moscow! But let my sin fall not on me, but thee, Boris, the regicide! Forward! Set on!

KURBSKY. Forward! Advance! And woe to Godunov.

(They gallop. The troops cross the frontier.)

THE COUNCIL OF THE TSAR

The TSAR, the PATRIARCH and Boyars

TSAR. Is it possible? An unfrocked monk against us Leads rascal troops, a truant friar dares write Threats to us! Then 'tis time to tame the madman! Trubetskoy, set thou forth, and thou Basmanov; My zealous governors need help. Chernigov Already by the rebel is besieged; Rescue the city and citizens.

BASMANOV. Three months Shall not pass, Sire, ere even rumour's tongue Shall cease to speak of the pretender; caged In iron, like a wild beast from oversea, We'll hale him into Moscow, I swear by God.

(Exit with TRUBETSKOY.)

TSAR. The Lord of Sweden hath by envoys tendered Alliance to me. But we have no need To lean on foreign aid; we have enough Of our own warlike people to repel Traitors and Poles. I have refused. — Shchelkalov! In every district to the governors Send edicts, that they mount their steeds, and send The people as of old on service; likewise Ride to the monasteries, and there enlist The servants of the churchmen. In days of old, When danger faced our country, hermits freely Went into battle; it is not now our wish To trouble them; no, let them pray for us; Such is the tsar's decree, such the resolve Of his boyars. And now a weighty question We shall determine; ye know how everywhere The insolent pretender hath spread abroad His artful rumours; letters everywhere, By him distributed, have sowed alarm And doubt; seditious whispers to and fro Pass in the market-places; minds are seething. We needs must cool them; gladly would I refrain From executions, but by what means and how? That we will now determine. Holy father, Thou first declare thy thought.

PATRIARCH. The Blessed One, The All-Highest, hath instilled into thy soul, Great lord, the spirit of kindness and meek patience; Thou wishest not perdition for the sinner, Thou wilt wait quietly, until delusion Shall pass away; for pass away it will, And truth's eternal sun will dawn on all. Thy faithful bedesman, one in worldly matters No prudent judge, ventures today to offer His voice to thee. This offspring of the devil, This unfrocked monk, has known how to appear Dimitry to the people. Shamelessly He clothed himself with

Boris Godunov: A Drama in Verse

the name of the tsarevich As with a stolen vestment. It only needs To tear it off—and he'll be put to shame By his own nakedness. The means thereto God hath Himself supplied. Know, sire, six years Since then have fled; 'twas in that very year When to the seat of sovereignty the Lord Anointed thee—there came to me one evening A simple shepherd, a venerable old man, Who told me a strange secret. "In my young days, " He said, "I lost my sight, and thenceforth knew not Nor day, nor night, till my old age; in vain I plied myself with herbs and secret spells; In vain did I resort in adoration To the great wonder-workers in the cloister; Bathed my dark eyes in vain with healing water From out the holy wells. The Lord vouchsafed not Healing to me. Then lost I hope at last, And grew accustomed to my darkness. Even Slumber showed not to me things visible, Only of sounds I dreamed. Once in deep sleep I hear a childish voice; it speaks to me: 'Arise, grandfather, go to Uglich town, To the Cathedral of Transfiguration; There pray over my grave. The Lord is gracious— And I shall pardon thee. ' 'But who art thou? ' I asked the childish voice. 'I am the tsarevich Dimitry, whom the Heavenly Tsar hath taken Into His angel band, and I am now A mighty wonder-worker. Go, old man. ' I woke, and pondered. What is this? Maybe God will in very deed vouchsafe to me Belated healing. I will go. I bent My footsteps to the distant road. I reached Uglich, repair unto the holy minster, Hear mass, and, glowing with zealous soul, I weep Sweetly, as if the blindness from mine eyes Were flowing out in tears. And when the people Began to leave, to my grandson I said: 'Lead me, Ivan, to the grave of the tsarevich Dimitry. ' The boy led me—and I scarce Had shaped before the grave a silent prayer, When sight illumed my eyeballs; I beheld The light of God, my grandson, and the tomb. " That is the tale, Sire, which the old man told.

(General agitation. In the course of this speech Boris several times wipes his face with his handkerchief.)

To Uglich then I sent, where it was learned That many sufferers had found likewise Deliverance at the grave of the tsarevich. This is my counsel; to the Kremlin send The sacred relics, place them in the Cathedral Of the Archangel; clearly will the people See then the godless villain's fraud; the might Of the fiends will vanish as a cloud of dust.

(Silence.)

PRINCE SHUISKY. What mortal, holy father, knoweth the ways Of the All-Highest? 'Tis not for me to judge Him. Untainted sleep and power of wonder-working He may upon the child's remains bestow; But vulgar rumour must dispassionately And diligently be tested; is it for us, In stormy times of insurrection, To weigh so great a matter? Will men not say That insolently we made of sacred things A worldly instrument? Even now the people Sway senselessly this way and that, even now There are enough already of loud rumours; This is no time to vex the people's minds With aught so unexpected, grave, and strange. I myself see 'tis needful to demolish The rumour spread abroad by the unfrocked monk; But for this end other and simpler means Will serve. Therefore, when it shall please thee, Sire, I will myself appear in public places, I will persuade, exhort away this madness, And will expose the vagabond's vile fraud.

TSAR. So be it! My lord Patriarch, I pray thee Go with us to the palace, where today I must converse with thee.

(Exeunt; all the boyars follow them.)

1ST BOYAR. (Sotto voce to another.) Didst mark how pale Our sovereign turned, how from his face there poured A mighty sweat?

2ND BOYAR. I durst not, I confess, Uplift mine eyes, nor breathe, nor even stir.

1ST BOYAR. Prince Shuisky has pulled it through. A splendid fellow!

Boris Godunov: A Drama in Verse

A PLAIN NEAR NOVGOROD SEVERSK

(DECEMBER 21st, 1604)

A BATTLE

SOLDIERS. (Run in disorder.) Woe, woe! The Tsarevich! The Poles! There they are! There they are!

(Captains enter: MARZHERET and WALTHER ROZEN.)

MARZHERET. Whither, whither? Allons! Go back!

ONE OF THE FUGITIVES. You go back, if you like, cursed infidel.

MARZHERET. Quoi, quoi?

ANOTHER. Kva! kva! You like, you frog from over the sea, to croak at the Russian tsarevich; but we—we are orthodox.

MARZHERET. Qu'est-ce a dire "orthodox"? Sacres gueux, maudite canaille! Mordieu, mein Herr, j'enrage; on dirait que ca n'a pas de bras pour frapper, ca n'a que des jambes pour fuir.

ROZEN. Es ist Schande.

MARZHERET. Ventre-saint gris! Je ne bouge plus d'un pas; puisque le vin est tire, il faut le boire. Qu'en dites-vous, mein Herr?

ROZEN. Sie haben Recht.

MARZHERET. Tudieu, il y fait chaud! Ce diable de "Pretender," comme ils l'appellent, est un bougre, qui a du poil au col? —Qu'en pensez-vous, mein Herr?

ROZEN. Ja.

MARZHERET. He! Voyez donc, voyez donc! L'action s'engage sur les derrieres de l'ennemi. Ce doit etre le brave Basmanov, qui aurait fait une sortie.

ROZEN. Ich glaube das.

(Enter Germans.)

MARZHERET. Ha, ha! Voici nos allemands. Messieurs! Mein Herr, dites-leur donc de se raillier et, sacrebleu, chargeons!

ROZEN. Sehr gut. Halt! (The Germans halt.) Marsch!

THE GERMANS. (They march.) Hilf Gott!

(Fight. The Russians flee again.)

POLES. Victory! Victory! Glory to the tsar Dimitry!

DIMITRY. (On horseback.) Cease fighting. We have conquered. Enough! Spare Russian blood. Cease fighting.

Boris Godunov: A Drama in Verse

OPEN SPACE IN FRONT OF THE CATHEDRAL IN MOSCOW

THE PEOPLE

ONE OF THE PEOPLE. Will the tsar soon come out of the Cathedral?

ANOTHER. The mass is ended; now the Te Deum is going on.

THE FIRST. What! Have they already cursed him?

THE SECOND. I stood in the porch and heard how the deacon cried out: —Grishka Otrepiev is anathema!

THE FIRST. Let him curse to his heart's content; the tsarevich has nothing to do with the Otrepiev.

THE SECOND. But they are now singing mass for the repose of the soul of the tsarevich.

THE FIRST. What? A mass for the dead sung for a living Man? They'll suffer for it, the godless wretches!

A THIRD. Hist! A sound. Is it not the tsar?

A FOURTH. No, it is the idiot.

(An idiot enters, in an iron cap, hung round with chains, surrounded by boys.)

THE BOYS. Nick, Nick, iron nightcap! T-r-r-r-r—

OLD WOMAN. Let him be, you young devils. Innocent one, pray thou for me a sinner.

IDIOT. Give, give, give a penny.

OLD WOMAN. There is a penny for thee; remember me in thy prayers.

IDIOT. (Seats himself on the ground and sings:)

> The moon sails on,
> The kitten cries,
> Nick, arise,
> Pray to God.

(The boys surround him again.)

ONE OF THEM. How do you do, Nick? Why don't you take off your cap?

(Raps him on the iron cap.)

How it rings!

IDIOT. But I have got a penny.

BOYS. That's not true; now, show it.

(They snatch the penny and run away.)

IDIOT. (Weeps.) They have taken my penny, they are hurting Nick.

THE PEOPLE. The tsar, the tsar is coming!

(The TSAR comes out from the Cathedral; a boyar in front of him scatters alms among the poor. Boyars.)

IDIOT. Boris, Boris! The boys are hurting Nick.

TSAR. Give him alms! What is he crying for?

IDIOT. The boys are hurting me... Give orders to slay them, as thou slewest the little tsarevich.

BOYARS. Go away, fool! Seize the fool!

TSAR. Leave him alone. Pray thou for me, Nick.

(Exit.)

IDIOT. (To himself.) No, no! It is impossible to pray for tsar Herod; the Mother of God forbids it.

SYEVSK

The PRETENDER, surrounded by his supporters

PRETENDER. Where is the prisoner?

A POLE. Here.

PRETENDER. Call him before me.

(A Russian prisoner enters.)

Who art thou?

PRISONER. Rozhnov, a nobleman of Moscow.

PRETENDER. Hast long been in the service?

PRISONER. About a month.

PRETENDER. Art not ashamed, Rozhnov, that thou hast drawn The sword against me?

PRISONER. What else could I do? 'Twas not our fault.

PRETENDER. Didst fight beneath the walls Of Seversk?

PRISONER. 'Twas two weeks after the battle I came from Moscow.

PRETENDER. What of Godunov?

PRISONER. The battle's loss, Mstislavsky's wound, hath caused him Much apprehension; Shuisky he hath sent To take command.

PRETENDER. But why hath he recalled Basmanov unto Moscow?

PRISONER. The tsar rewarded His services with honour and with gold. Basmanov in the council of the tsar Now sits.

PRETENDER. The army had more need of him. Well, how go things in Moscow?

PRISONER. All is quiet, Thank God.

PRETENDER. Say, do they look for me?

PRISONER. God knows; They dare not talk too much there now. Of some The tongues have been cut off, of others even The heads. It is a fearsome state of things— Each day an execution. All the prisons Are crammed. Wherever two or three forgather In public places, instantly a spy Worms himself in; the tsar himself examines At leisure the denouncers. It is just Sheer misery; so silence is the best.

PRETENDER. An enviable life for the tsar's people! Well, how about the army?

PRISONER. What of them? Clothed and full-fed they are content with all.

PRETENDER. But is there much of it?

PRISONER. God knows.

PRETENDER. All told Will there be thirty thousand?

PRISONER. Yes; 'twill run Even to fifty thousand.

(The Pretender reflects; those around him glance at one another.)

PRETENDER. Well! Of me What say they in your camp?

PRISONER. Your graciousness They speak of; say that thou, Sire, (be not wrath), Art a thief, but a fine fellow.

PRETENDER. (Laughing.) Even so I'll prove myself to them in deed. My friends, We will not wait for Shuisky; I wish you joy; Tomorrow, battle.

(Exit.)

ALL. Long life to Dimitry!

A POLE. Tomorrow, battle! They are fifty thousand, And we scarce fifteen thousand. He is mad!

ANOTHER. That's nothing, friend. A single Pole can challenge Five hundred Muscovites.

PRISONER. Yes, thou mayst challenge! But when it comes to fighting, then, thou braggart, Thou'lt run away.

POLE. If thou hadst had a sword, Insolent prisoner, then (pointing to his sword) with this I'ld soon Have vanquished thee.

PRISONER. A Russian can make shift Without a sword; how like you this (shows his fist), you fool?

(The Pole looks at him haughtily and departs in silence. All laugh.)

A FOREST

PRETENDER and PUSHKIN

(In the background lies a dying horse)

PRETENDER. Ah, my poor horse! How gallantly he charged Today in the last battle, and when wounded, How swiftly bore me. My poor horse!

PUSHKIN. (To himself.) Well, here's A great ado about a horse, when all Our army's smashed to bits.

PRETENDER. Listen! Perhaps He's but exhausted by the loss of blood, And will recover.

PUSHKIN. Nay, nay; he is dying.

PRETENDER. (Goes to his horse.) My poor horse! —what to do? Take off the bridle, And loose the girth. Let him at least die free.

(He unbridles and unsaddles the horse. Some Poles enter.)

Good day to you, gentlemen! How is't I see not Kurbsky among you? I did note today How to the thick of the fight he clove his path; Around the hero's sword, like swaying ears Of corn, hosts thronged; but higher than all of them His blade was brandished, and his terrible cry Drowned all cries else. Where is my knight?

POLE. He fell On the field of battle.

PRETENDER. Honour to the brave, And peace be on his soul! How few unscathed Are left us from the fight! Accursed Cossacks, Traitors and miscreants, you, you it is Have ruined us! Not even for three minutes To keep the foe at bay! I'll teach the villains! Every tenth man I'll hang. Brigands!

PUSHKIN. Whoe'er Be guilty, all the same we were clean worsted, Routed!

PRETENDER. But yet we nearly conquered. Just When I had dealt with their front rank, the Germans Repulsed us utterly. But they're fine fellows! By God! Fine fellows! I love them for it. From them I'll form an honourable troop.

PUSHKIN. And where Shall we now spend the night?

PRETENDER. Why, here, in the forest. Why not this for our night quarters? At daybreak We'll take the road, and dine in Rilsk. Good night.

(He lies down, puts a saddle under his head, and falls asleep.)

PUSHKIN. A pleasant sleep, tsarevich! Smashed to bits, Rescued by flight alone, he is as careless As a simple child; 'tis clear that Providence Protects him, and we, my friends, will not lose heart.

Boris Godunov: A Drama in Verse

MOSCOW. PALACE OF THE TSAR

BORIS. BASMANOV

TSAR. He is vanquished, but what profit lies in that? We are crowned with a vain conquest; he has mustered Again his scattered forces, and anew Threatens us from the ramparts of Putivl. Meanwhile what are our heroes doing? They stand At Krom, where from its rotten battlements A band of Cossacks braves them. There is glory! No, I am ill content with them; thyself I shall despatch to take command of them; I give authority not to birth, but brains. Their pride of precedence, let it be wounded! The time has come for me to hold in scorn The murmur of distinguished nobodies, And quash pernicious custom.

BASMANOV. Ay, my lord Blessed a hundredfold will be that day When fire consumes the lists of noblemen With their dissensions, their ancestral pride.

TSAR. That day is not far off; let me but first Subdue the insurrection of the people.

BASMANOV. Why trouble about that? The people always Are prone to secret treason; even so The swift steed champs the bit; so doth a lad Chafe at his father's ruling. But what then? The rider quietly controls the steed, The father sways the son.

TSAR. Sometimes the horse Doth throw the rider, nor is the son at all times Quite 'neath the father's will; we can restrain The people only by unsleeping sternness. So thought Ivan, sagacious autocrat And storm-subduer; so his fierce grandson thought. No, no, kindness is lost upon the people; Act well—it thanks you not at all; extort And execute—'twill be no worse for you.

(Enter a boyar.)

What now?

BOYAR. The foreign guests are come.

TSAR. I go To welcome them. Basmanov, wait, stay here; I still have need to speak: a word with thee.

(Exit.)

BASMANOV. High sovereign spirit! God grant he may subdue The accurst Otrepiev; and much, still much Of good he'll do for Russia. A great thought Within his mind has taken birth; it must not Be suffered to grow cold. What a career For me when the ancestral horn he breaks Of the nobility. I have no rivals In war. I shall stand closest to the throne— And it may chance— But what is that strange sound?

(Alarum. Boyars and court-attendants run in disorder, meet each other and whisper.)

ONE. Fetch a physician!

ANOTHER. Quickly to the Patriarch!

A THIRD. He calls for the tsarevich, the tsarevich!

A FOURTH. A confessor!

BASMANOV. What has happened?

A FIFTH AND SIXTH. The tsar is ill, The tsar is dying.

BASMANOV. Good God!

A FIFTH. Upon the throne He sat, and suddenly he fell; blood gushed From his mouth and ears.

(The TSAR is carried in on a chair. All the Tsar's household; all the boyars.)

TSAR. Let all depart—alone Leave the tsarevich with me. (All withdraw.) I am dying; Let us embrace. Farewell, my son; this hour Thou wilt begin to reign. —O God, my God! This hour I shall appear before Thy presence— And have no time to purge my soul with shrift. But yet, my son, I feel thou art dearer to me Than is my soul's salvation—be it so! A subject was I born; it seemed ordained That I should die a subject in obscurity. Yet I attained to sovereignty; but how? Ask not. Enough that thou art innocent. In justice now thou'lt reign; and I alone Am answerable for all to God. Dear son, Cherish no false delusion, of thy free will Blind not thyself. Stormy the days wherein Thou dost assume the crown. He is dangerous, This strange pretender; with a fearful name He is armed. For many a year experienced In rule, I could restrain revolt and treason; They quaked with fear before me; treachery Dared not to raise its voice; but thou, a boy, An inexperienced ruler, how wilt thou Govern amid the tempests, quench revolt, Shackle sedition? But God is great! He gives Wisdom to youth, to weakness strength. —Give ear; Firstly, select a steadfast counsellor, Of cool, ripe years, loved of the people, honoured Mid the boyars for birth and fame—even Shuisky. The army craves today a skilful leader; Basmanov send, and firmly bear the murmurs Of the boyars. Thou from thy early years Didst sit with me in council, thou dost know The formal course of government; change not Procedure. Custom is the soul of states. Of late I have been forced to reinstate Bans, executions—these thou canst rescind; And they will bless thee, as they blessed thy uncle When he obtained the throne of the Terrible. At the same time, little by little, tighten Anew the reins of government; now slacken; But let them not slip from thy hands. Be gracious, Accessible to foreigners, accept Their service trustfully. Preserve with strictness The Church's discipline. Be taciturn; The royal voice must never lose itself Upon the air in emptiness, but like A sacred bell must sound but to announce Some great disaster or great festival. Dear son, thou art approaching to those years When woman's beauty agitates our blood. Preserve, preserve the sacred purity Of innocence and proud shamefacedness; He, who through passion has been wont to wallow In vicious pleasures in his youthful days, Becomes in manhood bloodthirsty and surly; His mind untimely darkens. Of thy household Be always head; show honour to thy mother, But rule thy house thyself; thou art a man And tsar to boot. Be loving to thy sister— Thou wilt be left of her the sole protector.

FEODOR. (On his knees.) No, no; live on, my father, and reign long; Without thee both the folk and we will perish.

TSAR. All is at end for me—mine eyes grow dark, I feel the coldness of the grave—

(Enter the PATRIARCH and prelates; behind them all the boyars lead the TSARITSA by the hand; the TSAREVNA is sobbing.)

Who's there? Ah, 'tis the vestment—so! The holy tonsure— The hour has struck. The tsar becomes a monk, And the dark sepulchre will be my cell. Wait yet a little, my lord Patriarch, I still am tsar. Listen to me, boyars: To this my son I now commit the tsardom; Do homage to

Feodor. Basmanov, thou, And ye, my friends, on the grave's brink I pray you To serve my son with zeal and rectitude! As yet he is both young and uncorrupted. Swear ye?

BOYARS. We swear.

TSAR. I am content. Forgive me Both my temptations and my sins, my wilful And secret injuries. —Now, holy father, Approach thou; I am ready for the rite.

(The rite of the tonsure begins. The women are carried out swooning.)

A TENT

BASMANOV leads in PUSHKIN

BASMANOV. Here enter, and speak freely. So to me He sent thee.

PUSHKIN. He doth offer thee his friendship And the next place to his in the realm of Moscow.

BASMANOV. But even thus highly by Feodor am I Already raised; the army I command; For me he scorned nobility of rank And the wrath of the boyars. I have sworn to him Allegiance.

PUSHKIN. To the throne's lawful successor Allegiance thou hast sworn; but what if one More lawful still be living?

BASMANOV. Listen, Pushkin: Enough of that; tell me no idle tales! I know the man.

PUSHKIN. Russia and Lithuania Have long acknowledged him to be Dimitry; But, for the rest, I do not vouch for it. Perchance he is indeed the real Dimitry; Perchance but a pretender; only this I know, that soon or late the son of Boris Will yield Moscow to him.

BASMANOV. So long as I Stand by the youthful tsar, so long he will not Forsake the throne. We have enough of troops, Thank God! With victory I will inspire them. And whom will you against me send, the Cossack Karel or Mnishek? Are your numbers many? In all, eight thousand.

PUSHKIN. You mistake; they will not Amount even to that. I say myself Our army is mere trash, the Cossacks only Rob villages, the Poles but brag and drink; The Russians—what shall I say? —with you I'll not Dissemble; but, Basmanov, dost thou know Wherein our strength lies? Not in the army, no. Nor Polish aid, but in opinion— yes, In popular opinion. Dost remember The triumph of Dimitry, dost remember His peaceful conquests, when, without a blow The docile towns surrendered, and the mob Bound the recalcitrant leaders? Thou thyself Saw'st it; was it of their free-will our troops Fought with him? And when did they so? Boris Was then supreme. But would they now? —Nay, nay, It is too late to blow on the cold embers Of this dispute; with all thy wits and firmness Thou'lt not withstand him. Were't not better for thee To furnish to our chief a wise example, Proclaim Dimitry tsar, and by that act Bind him your friend for ever? How thinkest thou?

BASMANOV. Tomorrow thou shalt know.

PUSHKIN. Resolve.

BASMANOV. Farewell.

PUSHKIN. Ponder it well, Basmanov.

(Exit.)

BASMANOV. He is right. Everywhere treason ripens; what shall I do? Wait, that the rebels may deliver me In bonds to the Otrepiev? Had I not better Forestall the stormy onset of the flood, Myself to— ah! But to forswear mine oath! Dishonour to deserve from age to age! The trust of my young sovereign to requite With horrible betrayal! 'Tis a light thing For a disgraced exile to meditate Sedition and conspiracy; but I? Is it for me, the favourite of my lord? — But death—but power—the people's miseries...

(He ponders.)

Here! Who is there? (Whistles.) A horse here! Sound the muster!

PUBLIC SQUARE IN MOSCOW

PUSHKIN enters, surrounded by the people

THE PEOPLE. The tsarevich a boyar hath sent to us. Let's hear what the boyar will tell us. Hither! Hither!

PUSHKIN. (On a platform.) Townsmen of Moscow! The tsarevich Bids me convey his greetings to you. (He bows.) Ye know How Divine Providence saved the tsarevich From out the murderer's hands; he went to punish His murderer, but God's judgment hath already Struck down Boris. All Russia hath submitted Unto Dimitry; with heartfelt repentance Basmanov hath himself led forth his troops To swear allegiance to him. In love, in peace Dimitry comes to you. Would ye, to please The house of Godunov, uplift a hand Against the lawful tsar, against the grandson Of Monomakh?

THE PEOPLE. Not we.

PUSHKIN. Townsmen of Moscow! The world well knows how much ye have endured Under the rule of the cruel stranger; ban, Dishonour, executions, taxes, hardships, Hunger—all these ye have experienced. Dimitry is disposed to show you favour, Courtiers, boyars, state-servants, soldiers, strangers, Merchants—and every honest man. Will ye Be stubborn without reason, and in pride Flee from his kindness? But he himself is coming To his ancestral throne with dreadful escort. Provoke not ye the tsar to wrath, fear God, And swear allegiance to the lawful ruler; Humble yourselves; forthwith send to Dimitry The Metropolitan, deacons, boyars, And chosen men, that they may homage do To their lord and father.

(Exit. Clamour of the People.)

THE PEOPLE. What is to be said? The boyar spake truth. Long live Dimitry, our father!

A PEASANT ON THE PLATFORM. People! To the Kremlin! To the Royal palace! The whelp of Boris go bind!

THE PEOPLE. (Rushing in a crowd.) Bind, drown him! Hail Dimitry! Perish the race of Godunov!

Boris Godunov: A Drama in Verse

THE KREMLIN. HOUSE OF BORIS

A GUARD on the Staircase. FEODOR at a Window

BEGGAR. Give alms, for Christ's sake.

GUARD. Go away; it is forbidden to speak to the prisoners.

FEODOR. Go, old man, I am poorer than thou; thou art at liberty.

(KSENIA, veiled, also comes to the window.)

ONE OF THE PEOPLE. Brother and sister—poor children, like birds in a cage.

SECOND PERSON. Are you going to pity them? Accursed Family!

FIRST PERSON. The father was a villain, but the children are innocent.

SECOND PERSON. The apple does not fall far from the apple-tree.

KSENIA. Dear brother! Dear brother! I think the boyars are coming to us.

FEODOR. That is Golitsin, Mosalsky. I do not know the others.

KSENIA. Ah! Dear brother. my heart sinks.

(GOLITSIN, MOSALSKY, MOLCHANOV, and SHEREFEDINOV; behind them three archers.)

THE PEOPLE. Make way, make way; the boyars come. (They enter the house.)

ONE OF THE PEOPLE. What have they come for?

SECOND. Most like to make Feodor Godunov take the oath.

THIRD. Very like. Hark! What a noise in the house! What an uproar! They are fighting!

THE PEOPLE. Do you hear? A scream! That was a woman's voice. We will go up. We will go up! —The doors are fastened—the cries cease—the noise continues.

(The doors are thrown open. MOSALSKY appears on the staircase.)

MOSALSKY. People! Maria Godunov and her son Feodor have poisoned themselves. We have seen their dead bodies.

(The People are silent with horror.)

Why are ye silent? Cry, Long live the tsar Dimitry Ivanovich!

(The People are speechless.)

THE END

Lightning Source UK Ltd.
Milton Keynes UK
UKHW010648260720
367197UK00001B/49